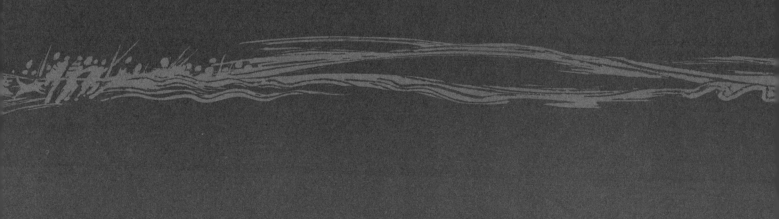

"We haven't seen even a lemming all day," Little Sister complained. She trudged across the tundra behind her older brother. "I'm tired. Let's go back to camp."

"First we will pick some more cranberries," Brother replied. "They are small, but they will keep us from starving."

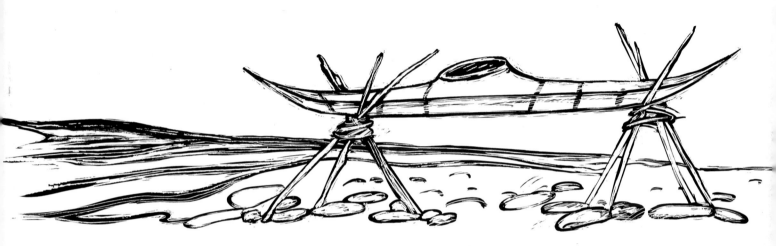

For many days, there had been no food in the Inuit camp where Brother and Little Sister lived. The two orphans had stayed with their aunt after the death of their parents. They had set out early that morning, hoping to find some food they could bring back to share with their people.

While they were away, the best hunter in the camp called the people together.

"We will go across the river," he said. "Perhaps the hunting will be better over there."

Quickly, the adults took down the tents. They rolled their belongings in caribou skins and slung them over their backs. With the children and dogs following behind, they started for the river.

In the confusion, no one noticed that Brother and Little Sister were missing.

When the two orphans returned, the campsite was deserted. Only a few small skins, a tangle of dog harnesses, and a broken trap marked where the tents had stood a short while before.

"Why did they go?" Little Sister cried in dismay. "Why have they left us behind?"

"Don't worry, my sister," said her brother. "We will catch up with them."

When the people reached the river, the men tied their kayaks together to make a raft to take their belongings to the other side.

They pushed the raft into the swirling river. The freezing water rose to their knees, then to their waists, and then to their chests as they waded beside the raft. At times they lost their footing, fought against the current, and slipped beneath the icy water. But finally they reached the other side.

The men made trip after trip until all their belongings were safely across the river. Then they began to ferry the women and children across on the raft.

Brother and Little Sister reached the river edge just after the last of the people left the shore.

A boy on the raft turned and saw the orphans. He cried, "It's Little Sister and Brother. We must go back for them."

But the eyes of the adults were fixed on the far shore. They did not hear the cries of the children over the rushing water.

"What are we going to do?" Little Sister cried as she watched the raft become smaller and smaller. "We are all alone."

"They will return for us," Brother replied. "But first we must find shelter for the night."

The two children returned to their old campsite and tried to find things they could use to make a shelter. Little Sister found a small piece of flint in a caribou bag, but all Brother found was a dried-out sealskin too small to make a tent.

"At least I can use your flint to start a fire," Brother said.

By the time the sky was dark, his fire burned brightly. The two children huddled beside the warm blaze and ate the cranberries they had picked early that morning. Brother wrapped the sealskin around his sister, and they watched the stars appear in the sky.

"We cannot survive alone," Brother said. "We must live with one of our animal cousins until our people return. What about Netsirq, the seal?"

"We cannot swim in the icy sea like Netsirq," Sister replied. "We do not have a thick layer of blubber to keep us warm."

"Tuktu, the caribou, will protect us," Brother suggested.

"Tuktu runs too swiftly," Little Sister replied. "We cannot keep up with him."

"We could live with *Nanook*, the bear," Brother said after some thought.

Little Sister shook her head. "I'm afraid of his sharp teeth and long claws. Besides, *Nanook* swims for miles in the ocean. We could never do that."

The night passed. Brother named all the animals he knew, but there was not one with whom they could live.

At last, Little Sister looked up at the stars. "We could live with the stars in the sky," she said.

"You are wise, little one," Brother replied. "We would be safe high above the Earth."

But, as the children joined hands and rose into the night sky, Little Sister cried out, "It's too dark up here. I'm afraid!"

"Strike a light with your flint," Brother replied.

    As the spark from his sister's flint shot across the sky, the boy laughed. The sealskin in his hand crackled loudly. It echoed across the tundra like a drum.

    "Do that again!" Little Sister exclaimed. She was no longer afraid.

    Through the night, Brother and Little Sister filled the sky with streaks of light and made the heavens roar.

When morning came, they curled up in the clouds and slept.

For many nights, the children played in the sky. They were so happy they forgot they had ever lived on Earth.

Then, one evening, Brother looked down on the place where their old camp had been. "Sister," he called, "our people have returned for us."

"Let's show them our new game," Little Sister exclaimed. Streaks of fire shot from her flint, and the tundra below echoed with the rumble of Brother's sealskin.

Fearfully, the people cried, "It's the orphans we came to find. See how powerful they are now."

Then they called Little Sister by the name of Lightning, and Brother they named Thunder. They begged the children to return to live with them.

"What shall we do, my sister?" Thunder asked.

The heavens were quiet as Lightning thought.

At last, she said, "On Earth, we were orphans. Up here, the sun is our father. The moon is our mother. The northern lights and the stars are our brothers and sisters. This is where we belong."

From then on, Thunder and Lightning made their home in the sky. But each autumn, when the heavens are filled with the crash of Brother's sealskin and the fire from Little Sister's flint, the people remember the two orphans who lived with them so long ago.

Northern Lights Books for Children are published by
Red Deer Press
813 MacKimmie Library Tower
2500 University Drive N.W.
Calgary Alberta Canada T2N 1N4
www.reddeerpress.com

Credits
Edited for the Press by Peter Carver
Cover and text design by Blair Kerrigan/Glyphics
Printed and bound in China by Stone Sapphire for Red Deer Press

Acknowledgments
Financial support provided by the Canada Council, the Department of Canadian Heritage, the Alberta Foundation for the
Arts, a beneficiary of the Lottery Fund of the Government of Alberta, and the University of Calgary.

ALBERTA Lotteries

The Alberta Foundation for the Arts

Alberta COMMUNITY DEVELOPMENT
COMMITTED TO THE DEVELOPMENT OF CULTURE AND THE ARTS

Canada

THE CANADA COUNCIL | LE CONSEIL DES ARTS
FOR THE ARTS | DU CANADA
SINCE 1957 | DEPUIS 1957

National Library of Canada Cataloguing in Publication Data

Bushey, Jeanne, 1944–
Orphans in the sky / Jeanne Bushey ; illustrated by Vladyana Krykorka.

(Northern lights books for children)
ISBN 0-88995-291-4

1. Inuit children—Juvenile fiction. I. Krykorka, Vladyana II. Title. III. Series.
PS8553.U69654O76 2004   jC813'.54   C2004-901671-7

5 4 3 2 1

The colour illustrations for *Orphans in the Sky* were painted in tempera on watercolour paper.
The black and white illustrations were done in India ink on scratchboard.

For Andrew and Richard
– Jeanne Bushey

To Jack Johnson, for transforming my life
– Vladyana Krykorka